Little Toot and the Loch Ness Monster

HARDIE GRAMATKY

with additional art by Dorothea Cooke Gramatky

Here's a big toot for all the students at Pingry School! Much love,

Dorothea Gramatky

&

Linda Gramatky Smith

5/16/92

G. P. Putnam's Sons · New York

Published simultaneously in Canada.
Printed in Hong Kong by South China Printing Co.
Library of Congress Cataloging-in-Publication Data
Gramatky, Hardie, 1907–1979
Little Toot and the Loch Ness Monster/by Hardie Gramatky;
illustrated by Hardie & Dorothea Gramatky. p.cm.
Summary: Little Toot travels to Scotland
where he befriends the Loch Ness monster.
[1. Tugboats—Fiction.   2. Loch Ness monster—Fiction.
3. Monsters—Fiction.]   I. Gramatky, Dorothea, ill.   II. Title.
PZ7.G7654Lid 1989   [E]—dc19   88-8504   CIP   AC
ISBN 0-399-21684-7
First impression

For Hardie,
whose presence in our lives
has enriched us all
—DCG & LGS

One night Little Toot had a dream. He dreamed he saw an enormous monster with large, bulging eyes and green scales. "It even had flippers and wings," he told the other riverboats.

"There are *no* monsters!" the riverboats jeered. All but Grandfather Toot. "I have heard of one fierce, awful monster," he said. "It lives in a lake called Loch Ness, far across the sea in Scotland. Go and find out for yourself," he told Little Toot.

"A waste of time," the riverboats said.

It seemed a long, long way to go, but Little Toot was determined to find the monster.

So, hiding his fears, the small tugboat bravely set off. He traveled across the ocean, through a narrow canal and past cliffs piled high with boulders. All the while he imagined what real monsters would look like.

He finally reached Loch Ness. The lake was
a spooky place with rolling hills and deep, dark
water sliced through by silver streaks of light.

Little Toot looked around...but he saw no
monsters anywhere. All he could see were the
ruins of a castle on a cliff high above Loch Ness.

Little Toot came upon a group of boats that were hunting for the Loch Ness monster. Wire mesh stretched across their bows like spider webs, and long, shiny arms reached out like feelers. From stem to stern their decks were loaded with strange contraptions.

They didn't want Little Toot around. "What do you think he's doing here?" one boat asked suspiciously. As Little Toot moved away, the search boats decided to find out if this new-comer knew any secrets.

Everywhere Little Toot went, the search boats followed. When he wandered around docks, they wandered around docks. When he got lost in dark coves, they went bleeping and blurping right behind him.

Then the little tugboat drifted into an underground tunnel beneath the old castle. "Get out!" they ordered Little Toot. "We'll search this cave ourselves."

The little tugboat chugged slowly back to the docks. He saw a Scottish fishing boat and thought, *Maybe he will talk to me.* But the old boat was in no mood to answer Little Toot's questions.

"Go away," he growled. "I dunna like all you boats pesterin' me. You've been annoying me for weeks."

"But, but…" Little Toot protested as the boat turned away.

Now Little Toot knew no one, anywhere. The loch was still and all the search boats had gone for the night.

He felt so alone.

As he floated along, thinking about home
and his dream, a light mist rose over the water.
Shadows appeared. They moved in and out.
Gray-green shapes huddled in small groups.
Were these monsters? Little Toot shivered.

Suddenly, he felt the shapes all around him, tugging and twisting. He was tossed high in the air, and as waves washed over him, Little Toot cried out, "Monsters!"

"Stop!" a voice shouted. "It's only the wind!" And there in front of Little Toot appeared a real live monster. It was huge and serpentlike with spines on its back.

"I am Nessie," the creature said softly. She smiled and blinked her eyes. "I've been watching you."

"But you're not a fierce-awful monster," Little Toot blurted out. Nessie laughed and darted out over the water.

She turned and swam in circles around the little tugboat. Not to be outdone by the playful monster, Little Toot joined in the fun. He couldn't wait to tell everyone at home that he had found the Loch Ness monster!

Little Toot showed Nessie how to make a perfect figure 8 as they glided together under a sky bright with stars. They laughed and giggled at each other's silly antics. The dark hills around the lake glowed a beautiful purple.

But as they got closer to the castle, the steep cliff cast dark shadows over the water, and even Nessie seemed nervous.

"Great green monsters once lived here," she whispered to Little Toot. "They had sharp, jagged teeth and bodies covered with scales."

Just like my dream, Little Toot thought.

"All the monsters are gone now. I'm the only one left," she went on, "so I am the one they are hunting. The whole world thinks I am a fierce-awful monster. But I'll tell you the truth — I'm afraid of being found. That's why I hide deep in the lake."

Afraid! Poor Nessie. Little Toot thought about the boats searching for her and how they would take her away from Loch Ness if they caught her.

"I was afraid, too," he told her. "Especially tonight when I thought the wind and waves were monsters coming after me."

Little Toot told Nessie about how he had come all the way across the ocean to find out if she were real.

The two friends talked all night. They didn't notice the sun had come up until they heard scary bleeping and blurping sounds through the mist.

Nessie frantically looked for a place to hide. In panic, she rushed into the dark tunnel under the castle. It was the worst thing she could have done. The search boats surrounded the cave.

Little Toot tried desperately to distract them by blowing smoke balls, but they pushed past him.

The small tugboat felt helpless. He had to think of something!

He looked up and high above him on the cliff even the boulders looked like monsters. That gave him an idea.

He hurled his towline up the cliff and it caught on a huge boulder. Little Toot pulled, and when his line was taut, he tugged with all his might. The boulder didn't budge. He thought of his friend Nessie and pulled again.

The boulder moved. It rolled slowly to the edge of the cliff...

. . . and Little Toot gave one last tug, hard as he could. *Splash!* The boulder hit the water and sent out shock waves all over the lake.

"The monster!" Little Toot shouted. "The Loch Ness monster has escaped!"

The search boats rushed out of the tunnel, panting and puffing, and raced off in the direction that Little Toot pointed. Out through the lochs, down the canal, out into the open sea.

When the old fishing boat saw the search boats leave, he praised Little Toot for being a hero. "Someday perhaps," he told Little Toot, "new boats will come a-pesterin'. But they'll never find Nessie."

It was time for Little Toot to go home. Nessie came out from her hiding place to say goodbye to her friend, and Little Toot blew her a small toot-toot as he headed toward the sea.

When Little Toot arrived home, the river-boats gathered around to ask, "Well, did you find the Loch Ness monster?"

Little Toot thought of Nessie and smiled. "What Loch Ness monster?" he replied, knowing that he'd always keep her secret.

After my father died in 1979 at the age of 72, our family's sadness was tempered by a feeling of joy that he would live on in the hearts of people who loved his *Little Toot* books.

Recently, as we became excited about the upcoming fiftieth anniversary of the publication of the original *Little Toot*, we felt it was time for us to complete my dad's last book, *Little Toot and the Loch Ness Monster*. He had left several drafts of the manuscript, notebooks bulging with his ideas and sketches for the book, and a number of the illustrations.

As a labor of love, our family has finished what Hardie Gramatky created. My mother, Dorothea Cooke Gramatky, an artist in her own right, did two illustrations based on his sketches and she added color to several black-and-white drawings. I worked on the manuscript, always thinking of this little tugboat as being an extension of my dad's personality. My husband, Kendall, and our children, Andrew and Tina, gave their reader's reactions just as they always did for my father over the years.

There has been a wonderful feeling of my dad's presence in this process, and we hope that you, the reader, will feel that love and creativity.

— *Linda Gramatky Smith*